The

D0863227

Samuel D. Hunter

A SAMUEL FRENCH ACTING EDITION

SAMUEL
FRENCH
FOUNDED 1830

SAMUELFRENCH.COM
SAMUELFRENCH-LONDON.CO.UK

MUSIC USE NOTE

Licensees are solely responsible for obtaining formal written permission from copyright owners to use copyrighted music in the performance of this play and are strongly cautioned to do so. If no such permission is obtained by the licensee, then the licensee must use only original music that the licensee owns and controls. Licensees are solely responsible and liable for all music clearances and shall indemnify the copyright owners of the play(s) and their licensing agent, Samuel French, against any costs, expenses, losses and liabilities arising from the use of music by licensees. Please contact the appropriate music licensing authority in your territory for the rights to any incidental music.

IMPORTANT BILLING AND CREDIT REQUIREMENTS

If you have obtained performance rights to this title, please refer to your licensing agreement for important billing and credit requirements.

THE WHALE was first produced by the Denver Center Theatre Company at the Ricketson Theatre in Denver, Colorado on January 19, 2012. The play was directed by Hal Brooks, with sets by Jason Simms, costumes by Kevin Copenhaver, lighting by Seth Reiser, sound by William Burns, dramaturgy by Mead Hunter, and fight direction by Geoffrey Kent. The cast was as follows:

CHARLIE. . . . . Tom Alan Robbins

LIZ . . . . Angela Reed

ELDER THOMAS. . . . . Cory Michael Smith

ELLIE. . . . . Nicole Rodenburg

MARY. . . . . Tasha Lawrence

THE WHALE was then produced by Playwrights Horizons at the Peter Jay Sharp Theater in New York City on October 12, 2012. The play was directed by Davis McCallum, with sets by Mimi Lien, costumes by Jessica Pabst, lighting by Jane Cox, sound by Fitz Patton, and dramaturgy by John M. Baker. The cast was as follows:

CHARLIE. . . . . Shuler Hensley

LIZ . . . . Cassie Beck/Rebecca Henderson

ELDER THOMAS. . . . . Cory Michael Smith

ELLIE. . . . . .Reyna de Courcy

MARY. . . . . Tasha Lawrence

CHARACTERS

CHARLIE – early to mid forties, male, weighing around 600 lbs

LIZ – mid to late thirties, female

ELDER THOMAS – 19, male.

ELLIE – 17, female.

MARY – early to mid forties, female

SETTING

Northern Idaho.

The main room of a small, white-walled, desolate apartment in a cheaply constructed two story building. The room is dominated by a large couch that sags in the middle, re-enforced by several cinder blocks.

Within arm's reach of the couch are: a small computer desk on rollers with a laptop on top, a large pile of papers, a walker, a claw for reaching, and a whole universe of full, empty, and half empty food containers (donuts, candy bars, fried chicken, burgers, two liter soda bottles, etc.). Little effort has been made to clean up trash or organize.

A small kitchen is off to one corner of the stage, a bathroom and bedroom offstage.

TIME

The Present.

AUTHOR'S NOTES

The play is served much better by being performed without an intermission (running time is roughly 1 hour, 50 minutes). However, if absolutely necessary, an intermission can be taken in between Wednesday night and Thursday morning.

Dialogue written in *italics* is emphatic, slow, deliberate; dialogue written in ALL CAPS is impulsive, quick, explosive.

A "/" indicates an overlap in dialogue.

For John

MONDAY

Morning.

(CHARLIE, a morbidly obese man in his early forties, dressed in oversized sweatpants and an oversized sweatshirt, sits on the couch in front of his laptop, speaking into a small microphone hooked up to his computer.)

CHARLIE. This is from a paper I got from a student last year, a freshman at UC Santa Barbara. He was writing this for an American Lit class. It's a paper about *The Great Gatsby*.

(pulling out an essay)

"There were many aspects to the book *The Great Gatsby*. But I was bored by it because it was about people that I don't care about and they do things I don't understand. In conclusion, *The Great Gatsby* wasn't so great, LOL."

(stops reading)

The problems with this essay are painfully obvious. The student has no discernible thesis, almost no analysis whatsoever... I'll be posting the paper in it's entirety, what I want you to do is read through it a few times, and then post a three to four paragraph response providing concrete ideas for revision. Also, those of you who haven't given me paper four, I need it by five o'clock, *no exceptions*. And remember – the more revision you guys do on these papers, the better. The more you can change, chances are the stronger these papers will be. Alright?

Afternoon.

(CHARLIE, in the same position before, in front of his computer, masturbating to gay porn.)

(After a few moments, his breathing becomes more and more shallow. He pushes the computer desk away from him. He feels some sharp pain in his chest.)

(He reaches toward his cell phone, but accidentally knocks it onto the floor. The pain becomes worse. All the while, the gay porn is still playing in the background.)

(CHARLIE takes some deep breaths, wheezing loudly, trying to calm himself down.)

(a knock at the door)

CHARLIE. Liz?!

(another knock)

It's not locked, just come in! I need help, I – !

(ELDER THOMAS enters, wearing a white shirt, black tie, and black slacks. He holds some books and a bike helmet.)

ELDER THOMAS. Oh, my God. Oh, Gosh, are you – ?

(pause)

I should call an ambulance. Should I call an ambulance?

(ELDER THOMAS notices the gay porn, still playing. CHARLIE quickly reaches over and shuts his laptop.)

I don't have a phone, do you have – ?

(CHARLIE pulls out a few sheets of paper, hands them to ELDER THOMAS.)

CHARLIE. Read this to me.

ELDER THOMAS. Wait, what?

CHARLIE. Read it to me, *please.*

ELDER THOMAS. I have to call you an ambulance! I don't know what to do, I'm just –

CHARLIE. I don't know what's going to happen in the next five minutes. Please, read it to me. PLEASE JUST READ IT TO ME.

ELDER THOMAS. OKAY! OKAY, I JUST –

(reading, quickly)

"In the amazing book *Moby Dick* by the author Herman Melville, the author recounts his story of being at sea. In the first part of his book, the author, calling himself Ishmael, is in a small sea-side town and he is sharing a bed with a man named Queequeg – "

(stops)

What is this?! Why am I reading this?! I need to call someone – !

CHARLIE. *(pleading)* PLEASE JUST READ IT. *ANY OF IT.*

ELDER THOMAS. *(reading)* "I was very saddened by this book, and I felt many emotions for the characters. And I felt saddest of all when I read the boring chapters that were only descriptions of whales, because I knew that the author was just trying to save us from his own sad story, just for a little while. This book made me think about my own life, and then it… It made me feel… "

*(**CHARLIE**'s breathing starts to become normal. He takes a few deep breaths, calming himself down.)*

Did that – help?

CHARLIE. Yes. Yes, it did.

ELDER THOMAS. I'm calling an ambulance, where's your phone?

CHARLIE. I don't go to hospitals.

ELDER THOMAS. I can't help you, I don't even know CPR – !

CHARLIE. *I don't go to hospitals.*

(pause)

I'm sorry. Excuse me, I'm sorry. You can go if you want, I… Thank you for reading that to me.

*(Pause. **ELDER THOMAS** doesn't move.)*

ELDER THOMAS. Are you feeling better?

CHARLIE. Yes.

ELDER THOMAS. Are you sure?

CHARLIE. Yes.

ELDER THOMAS. Okay. Um. I –

> *(pause)*

> I represent the Church of Jesus Christ of Latter Day Saints? We're sharing a message for all faiths?

CHARLIE. Oh.

ELDER THOMAS. Yeah.

> *(pause)*

> Would you – like to hear about the Church?

> *(pause)*

CHARLIE. Okay.

ELDER THOMAS. Really?

CHARLIE. Yes. Actually, yes.

> *(pause)*

> But I should call my friend. My friend is a nurse. She should come over. She knows what to do, she – takes care of me.

ELDER THOMAS. Okay, good, where's your – ?

CHARLIE. My cell phone is over there, can you get it for me?

> *(CHARLIE points to a cell phone on the other side of the room. ELDER THOMAS picks up the cell phone and hands it to CHARLIE.)*

ELDER THOMAS. Do you want me to – … ?

CHARLIE. Stay with me.

> *(pause)*

ELDER THOMAS. I really should –

CHARLIE. I'm not sure what's going to happen right now. I'd – rather there was someone here with me. If that's alright.

ELDER THOMAS. Yeah, okay.

CHARLIE. Thank you.

(*pause*)

ELDER THOMAS. What was – ? That thing I read to you about *Moby Dick*?

CHARLIE. It was an essay. It's my job, I do online tutoring, online classes on expository writing.

ELDER THOMAS. But why did you want me to read that to you?

CHARLIE. Because I thought I was dying. And I wanted to hear it one last time.

Later that Afternoon.

(CHARLIE sits on the couch, LIZ stands over him, taking his blood pressure. ELDER THOMAS sits in the corner.)

LIZ. You should have called an ambulance.

CHARLIE. With no health insurance?

LIZ. Being in debt is better than being dead. What's wrong with you? Why is there a Mormon here?

CHARLIE. Did I have a heart attack?

LIZ. No, you didn't have a heart attack.

(reading his blood pressure)

Huh.

CHARLIE. What is it?

(pause)

LIZ. Tell me what you felt.

CHARLIE. Pain, in my chest. It was hard to breathe, I felt like I couldn't intake air.

LIZ. How are you sleeping?

CHARLIE. I'm tired all the time. I'm sleeping on the couch now actually, I can breathe better.

(LIZ takes out a stethoscope. She checks his breathing.)

LIZ. You're wheezing.

CHARLIE. I always wheeze, Liz.

LIZ. You're wheezing more. Take a deep breath.

(CHARLIE takes a deep breath.)

LIZ. Did that hurt?

CHARLIE. A little. What was my blood pressure?

LIZ. 238 over 134.

(Pause. LIZ puts the stethoscope away.)

CHARLIE. Oh.

LIZ. Yeah. Oh.

(pause)

CHARLIE. Could you hand me my walker? I haven't been to the bathroom all day, I'm ready to explode.

*(**LIZ** hands him his walker, **CHARLIE** gets up with some effort. It's obvious he's having chest pain.)*

*(**LIZ** watches him.)*

LIZ. You want help?

CHARLIE. No, I'm fine. Just – . Sorry.

LIZ. What are you sorry about?

CHARLIE. Sorry. I don't know. Sorry.

*(**CHARLIE** makes his way to the bathroom, wheezing loudly.)*

*(**ELDER THOMAS** and **LIZ** look at one another.)*

ELDER THOMAS. I should go.

LIZ. Thank you. For helping him.

(pause)

You on your mission?

ELDER THOMAS. What?

LIZ. Is this your mission? You're on your mission now?

ELDER THOMAS. Oh – yeah.

LIZ. Where are you from?

ELDER THOMAS. Iowa.

LIZ. You grew up in Iowa and they sent you to *Idaho* on your mission?

ELDER THOMAS. Yeah, I don't know. Some of my friends got to go to Los Angeles. A few went to South America. It's – fine.

(pause)

Is he going to be – ?

LIZ. No. No, he's not.

ELDER THOMAS. He's sick?

LIZ. He's very, very, very sick.

(*pause*)

I grew up Mormon.

ELDER THOMAS. Really? Oh, that's – that's actually nice to hear, I actually haven't run into a lot of others. Surprising, small town in Idaho, you'd think you'd… Do you go to the church over near the highway, or the – ?

LIZ. I fucking hate Mormons.

(*small pause*)

I shouldn't say that, I don't fucking hate Mormons, I fucking hate Mormon*ism*. How can you believe in a God like that? He gives us the Old Testament, fine, we'll all be Jews. Then Jesus shows up and he's like, "Hey so, I'm the son of God, stop being Jewish, here's the New Testament, sorry." And then he shows up a *second* time, and he's like, "Oh, shit, sorry! Here's this other thing, it's called the Book of Mormon." And after all that, we're still supposed to wait around for him to come back a *third fucking time* to kill us all with holy fire and dragons and –

ELDER THOMAS. That's a really unfair summary of my beliefs.

LIZ. I'm just saying, why would God not just give us all the right answers to begin with?

ELDER THOMAS. He has a plan.

LIZ. A plan that he's constantly revising.

ELDER THOMAS. I guess.

(*pause*)

LIZ. Look – it was good of you to stay with him. But if you're waiting around to convert him, or –

ELDER THOMAS. We don't "convert people". Our message is a message of hope for / people of all faiths –

LIZ. People of all faiths, I know, you're sweet. But he's not interested in what you have to say. It's the last thing he wants to hear.

(lights up a cigarette)

Listen, you can go if you want. I know Charlie appreciates what you did.

ELDER THOMAS. He said he wanted to hear about the church.

(pause)

LIZ. Charlie said he wanted to hear about the church?

ELDER THOMAS. Yes.

(pause)

LIZ. No, he doesn't.

ELDER THOMAS. Why not?

LIZ. I just know.

ELDER THOMAS. How?

LIZ. Because it's caused him a lot of pain.

ELDER THOMAS. How?

LIZ. It killed his boyfriend.

(pause)

ELDER THOMAS. You're saying the church –

LIZ. – killed his boyfriend. Yes, the Church of Jesus Christ of Latter Day Saints killed Charlie's boyfriend.

(pause)

And I should add that, personally, the Mormon Church has caused *me* a lot of pain in *my* life. That guy in there is the only person I have any more that even resembles a friend, and I am not letting you come over here to talk to him. Especially not now, not this week.

ELDER THOMAS. Why not this week?

LIZ. Because he's probably not going to be here next week.

ELDER THOMAS. Where is he going?

(CHARLIE comes back out from the bathroom on his walker, moves toward the couch.)

CHARLIE. I'm sorry you had to come over, Liz. And I'm sorry –

LIZ. It's alright.

CHARLIE. I'm sorry that I always think I'm dying.

(pause)

LIZ. Charlie, your blood pressure is 238 over 134.

CHARLIE. That's not much more than it usually is.

LIZ. Yes, it is. And your normal blood pressure is at near-fatal levels as it is.

(pause)

CHARLIE. I'm sorry, I'm feeling better now. You can go back to –

LIZ. Go to the hospital.

CHARLIE. I'm sorry.

LIZ. Stop saying you're sorry. Go to the hospital.

CHARLIE. Liz – I'm sorry –

LIZ. I'm calling an ambulance and they're going to take you to the hospital!

CHARLIE. I can't!

LIZ. You're going to die, Charlie. You have congestive heart failure. If you don't go to the hospital, you will die. Probably before the weekend. You. Will. Die.

(pause)

CHARLIE. Then I should probably keep working, I have a lot of essays this week.

LIZ. GODAMMIT CHARLIE.

CHARLIE. I'm sorry. I'm sorry. I know, I'm – an awful person. I know. I'm sorry.

(pause)

ELDER THOMAS. Do you still want to hear about the church?

LIZ. NO. HE DOES NOT.

ELDER THOMAS. Okay. That's fine, I'm sorry, I – I'll go.

(*pause*)

I still don't understand why you wanted me to read that essay to you.

(*pause*)

CHARLIE. It's a really good essay.

ELDER THOMAS. I actually thought it was pretty bad.

CHARLIE. It got a bad grade. But – it's a really, really good essay.

(**ELDER THOMAS** *exits. A few beats pass.*)

LIZ. Did you tell him you wanted to hear about the Church?

CHARLIE. He's just a kid, Liz. He helped me out.

(**CHARLIE** *grunts in pain, holding his chest a bit.*)

LIZ. What?

CHARLIE. I'm fine.

LIZ. No, you're not.

(*pause*)

CHARLIE. I think – I need to call Ellie.

LIZ. Ellie?

CHARLIE. Yeah.

(*pause*)

LIZ. What, so you're like – giving up?

CHARLIE. What else am I supposed to do?

LIZ. Go to the hospital!

CHARLIE. Okay, I could go to the hospital. Get a bypass operation or whatever. Rack up several hundred thousand dollars of hospital bills that I won't be able to pay back, ever. Then I'll come back home, maybe, and last – what? A year? At the most? All so I could spend another year in what I'm sure is no small amount of pain.

LIZ. Nice positive thinking, Charlie. This affects me too, you know? You're my *friend*.

CHARLIE. I know. I'm sorry.

LIZ. You say you're sorry again, I'm going to shove a knife right into you, I swear to –

CHARLIE. Go ahead, what's it gonna do? My internal organs are two feet in at least.

(*Pause.* LIZ *laughs.*)

LIZ. Fuck you.

(**CHARLIE** *smiles. They look at one another.*)

(*Pause. Finally* LIZ *sighs, goes to the couch, grabbing the remote. She sits next to* **CHARLIE**, *puts her head on his shoulder.*)

(*She turns on the television, flips through the channels absent mindedly.*)

LIZ. I've been telling you that this was gonna happen.

CHARLIE. Yeah.

LIZ. Haven't I been telling you – ?

CHARLIE. Yes, I know. You have.

(*pause*)

LIZ. Well I'm not letting you just *die*. I don't care what you think, I'm not letting it happen.

(**LIZ** *continues to flip through the channels. Silence.*)

CHARLIE. Did you bring food?

(*Silence.* LIZ *continues to flip channels.*)

Liz.

(**LIZ** *flips a few more channels. Silence.*)

Please.

(*A few more channels. Silence. Then, without looking at* **CHARLIE**, **LIZ** *goes to her bag and pulls out a large bucket of fried chicken. She puts the chicken in* **CHARLIE**'s *lap, keeping her eyes on the television.*)

Thank you.

(**CHARLIE** *opens up the bucket, takes out some chicken, starts eating.* **LIZ** *continues to flip channels, then lands on one.*)

LIZ. Judge Judy, I've seen this one. It's good.

(**CHARLIE** *continues to eat,* **LIZ** *watches the television.*)

Night.

*(**CHARLIE**, alone, much later that night. The television is on at a low level. As he finishes, he turns off the TV, staring forward silently for a moment.)*

CHARLIE. *(soft)* In the first part of his book, the author, calling himself Ishmael, is in a small sea-side town and he is sharing a bed with a man named Queequeg.

*(**CHARLIE** takes a breath, tries to make himself comfortable on the couch.)*

The author and Queequeg go to church and hear a sermon about Jonah, and later set out on a ship captained by the pirate named Ahab, who is missing a leg, and very much wants to kill the whale which is named Moby Dick, and which is white.

*(**CHARLIE** breathes. He shifts on the couch, the movement causing pain in is chest.)*

In the course of the book, the pirate Ahab encounters many hardships. His entire life is set around trying to kill a certain whale. I think this is sad because this whale doesn't have any emotions, and doesn't know how bad Ahab wants to kill him.

*(**CHARLIE**'s settles into the couch, closes his eyes.)*

He's just a poor big animal. And I feel bad for Ahab as well, because he thinks that his life will be better if he can kill this whale, but in reality it won't help him at all. This book me made think about my own life. This book made me think about my own life. This book made me –

(Lights quickly snap to black.)

(In the darkness, there is the faint sound of waves lapping against the shore – so quiet that it's nearly indistinguishable. The sound continues for a moment, rising just a bit in volume, becoming a bit more discernible, before lights rise on:)

TUESDAY

Morning.

(CHARLIE sits on the couch. ELLIE stands near the door. There is an awkward silence.)

ELLIE. How much?

CHARLIE. I haven't been able to weigh myself in years, it's hard to know. Five-fifty? Six hundred?

ELLIE. That's disgusting.

CHARLIE. I know. It is disgusting, I'm sorry.

ELLIE. Does this mean I'm going to get fat?

CHARLIE. No, it doesn't. I was always big, but I just – let it get out of control.

(Pause.)

ELLIE. Who was the woman?

CHARLIE. What woman?

ELLIE. There was a woman in the background, when you called me.

CHARLIE. Oh, that's – my friend, Liz.

ELLIE. You have a friend?

CHARLIE. Yeah. She's a nurse, she used to do in-house calls for the hospice –

ELLIE. Is she, like, your fag hag? Because it seems like she could do a lot better.

(Pause.)

CHARLIE. Was your mom okay with you coming here?

ELLIE. I didn't tell her. She would've freaked out.

(pause)

Why don't you just go to the hospital?

CHARLIE. I don't have health insurance.

ELLIE. But you might die.

CHARLIE. It's not worth it.

(*pause*)

It's really good to see you. You look beautiful. How's school going? You're a senior, right?

ELLIE. You actually care?

CHARLIE. Of course I care. I pester your mom for information as often as she'll give it to me.

(*pause*)

So why aren't – don't you have school?

ELLIE. Suspended until Friday.

CHARLIE. Oh. Why?

ELLIE. I blogged about my stupid bitch lab partner. She told her stupid bitch mom and the vice principal said it was "vaguely threatening".

CHARLIE. You don't like high school?

ELLIE. Only retards like high school.

CHARLIE. But – you're going to pass, right?

ELLIE. I'm failing most of my classes. My dumbass counselor says I might not graduate. I'm a smart person, I never forget anything. But high school is such bullshit. Busywork.

CHARLIE. It's important.

ELLIE. How would you know?

(*pause*)

So, what? You want me to like help you clean yourself or go to the bathroom or something? Because if you need someone to help you do that stuff, then you need to find someone else.

CHARLIE. You don't need to do anything disgusting, I promise.

ELLIE. Just being around you is disgusting. You smell disgusting. Your apartment is disgusting. You look disgusting. The last time I saw you, you were disgusting.

CHARLIE. There's no way you could remember that. You were two years old.

ELLIE. I'm a smart person, I never forget anything. In the living room, with that old red couch and the TV with the wood frame. And you were on the floor, and mom was screaming at you and you were just apologizing over and over, you were so pathetic. I remember that. Can I have one of those donuts?

(small pause)

CHARLIE. Yeah, sure.

*(**ELLIE** grabs a donut from a package sitting near the kitchen.)*

ELLIE. You weren't all that heavy back then. I mean, you were fat, but not like this.

CHARLIE. Yeah.

ELLIE. Why did you gain all that weight?

(pause)

CHARLIE. I'd like us to spend some time together this week.

ELLIE. Why?

CHARLIE. We don't even know one another.

ELLIE. So?

(pause)

CHARLIE. I can pay you.

ELLIE. You want to pay me to spend time with you?

CHARLIE. And I can help you with your work. It's what I do for my job, I help people edit their essays –

ELLIE. Are you serious?

*(**CHARLIE** picks up some essays sitting next to him.)*

CHARLIE. It's what I do all day long. I can help you pass your classes.

ELLIE. How are you like, qualified to edit essays?

CHARLIE. I have a masters degree. In English, from the U of I. I teach online classes, it's my job.

ELLIE. You teach online?

CHARLIE. Yes.

ELLIE. Your students know what you look like?

(*pause*)

CHARLIE. I don't use a camera. Just a microphone.

ELLIE. That's probably a good idea.

(*pause*)

Counselor dumbass says that if I show a lot of improvement in one subject that I might be able to pass. I can rewrite my old essays for credit, so you have to rewrite all of those, and write every other essay for the rest of the semester. And they have to be really good.

CHARLIE. I really shouldn't write them for you.

ELLIE. Well, it's what you're gonna do if you want me around. How much can you pay me?

CHARLIE. Whatever I have. All the money I have in the bank.

ELLIE. How much money do you have in the bank?

(*pause*)

CHARLIE. A hundred and twenty –

ELLIE. You want me to be here all week for a hundred and twenty dollars?

CHARLIE. Thousand. A hundred and twenty thousand dollars.

(*pause*)

I never go out, I don't have health insurance, all I pay for is food, internet, three-fifty a month in rent. And I work all the time.

ELLIE. You'd give all that money to *me*? Not my mom, to *me*?

CHARLIE. Yes. All of it. Just – don't mention it to your mom. Okay?

(pause)

Also… I'll write the essays for you, but I'd like you to do some writing yourself. Just for me. They don't have to be perfect, I'd just like you to write an essay or two for me.

ELLIE. Why?

CHARLIE. You're a smart person, I bet you're a strong writer. I want to know what you have to say. Plus, I'm a teacher. I want to make sure you're getting something out of this.

ELLIE. I don't even understand you.

(silence)

Stand up and walk over to me.

CHARLIE. What?

ELLIE. Come over here. Walk toward me. Come over here, beside me.

*(**CHARLIE** pauses for a second, then reaches for his walker.)*

ELLIE. Without that thing. Just stand up, and come over here.

CHARLIE. Ellie, I can't really –

ELLIE. Shut up. Come over here.

*(**CHARLIE** takes a few deep breaths, then tries to stand on his feet.)*

(He is unsuccessful at getting off the couch, his chest pain becoming severe. His breathing becomes quicker.)

(He tries again, this time he nearly gets up on his feet, but falls backward when the pain becomes unbearable. He is wincing from the pain, lying back on the couch, wheezing loudly.)

*(**ELLIE** stares at him, unmoved.)*

Night.

(**CHARLIE** *sits on the couch.* **LIZ** *is standing near* **CHARLIE** *fiddling with a small machine with electrodes attached to it.*)

(**LIZ** *has brought various bulk-sized groceries, they sit near the door still in bags.*)

LIZ. I don't remember what it's called, something ridiculous, I don't remember. But it's for you, it's going to help you out. This machine here, it senses perspiration. It's an indicator of stress. So the idea is, if you know what makes your stress level go up, you can learn to control it. And that'll reduce your heart rate, lower your blood pressure.

(**LIZ** *starts attaching the machine to* **CHARLIE**'s *hand.*)

CHARLIE. Where did you get this thing?

LIZ. Ginny, from the hospital, she's into this stuff.

CHARLIE. Do you know how to use it?

LIZ. If Ginny can figure it out, I'm sure it's not that hard. Here.

(turns on the machine)

You see that number right there? That's how much you're sweating. You wanna try and take that number go down.

(pause)

CHARLIE. So what do I – ?

LIZ. I don't know, just – relax. Take a deep breath. You're calm. You're very, very calm.

(**CHARLIE** *takes a deep breath.* **LIZ** *rubs his shoulders a bit, watching the machine.*)

LIZ. There, the number's going down. Isn't that better? It's about establishing a relationship between your brain and your body. Now you know you're calming yourself down because the little machine is telling you so.

CHARLIE. You really think this is going to help?

LIZ. Yes! It'll help, you just – need to do this all the time.

*(Pause. **LIZ** continues to rub his shoulders and watch the machine.)*

CHARLIE. Ellie came over.

(pause)

LIZ. She did?

CHARLIE. Yes.

(pause)

She's – amazing.

LIZ. Yeah?

CHARLIE. And – angry. Very angry. She's coming back tomorrow. I'm writing her essays for her, for school. She's failing most of her classes, I think. She's smart, I can tell she's smart, she just doesn't –

LIZ. Charlie, do you really – ? You really think this is a good idea?

CHARLIE. What do you mean?

LIZ. Sorry, but you haven't seen this girl since she was two years old, and *now* you want to reconnect with her? By doing her homework for her?

CHARLIE. It's fine. It'll be fine.

LIZ. What is she gonna do if something happens to you, if you need help?

CHARLIE. I just want to spend some time with her, get to know her. I'm – worried about her.

LIZ. Why?

CHARLIE. She has this – website.

*(**CHARLIE** opens up his laptop, pulls up a website.)*

*(**LIZ** looks at the computer.)*

LIZ. I don't understand, what am I looking at?

CHARLIE. She calls it a "hate blog". She posts pictures of her friends, her mom even, and she just – insults them. The only thing she ever talks about is how much she doesn't like people.

LIZ. Huh. She's an angry little girl.

CHARLIE. Yes, she is. And I'm worried.

LIZ. She's just being a teenager. She'll be fine, she's got her mom to look out for her.

(*LIZ goes to her shopping bags, puts the food away in the kitchen as she talks.*)

LIZ. Listen, you shouldn't worry about her. When I was a kid – when my dad would really piss me off – I used to go to the supermarket over on Johnson, you remember that big place that used to be out there?

CHARLIE. Sure.

LIZ. I used to just – *trash* the place. And I was really good at it, I never got caught. I'd walk in really normally, wait until I was in an aisle with no one in it, and then I'd – very quietly – destroy it. Open all the jars and boxes, spill everything on the floor. Pour out the milk, smash the produce under my feet. By the time I was done, they didn't know what hit them. Like this silent tornado had swept through the whole store. I was one angry little girl.

CHARLIE. You never told me about that.

LIZ. Yeah, well, it's not exactly a time in my life I love to think about, or – .

(*pause*)

I'm just saying, you should be thankful that Ellie's doing this shit on the internet and not getting herself into real trouble.

(*LIZ takes an extra large meatball sub out of a shopping bag, brings it to* **CHARLIE**. **CHARLIE** *starts eating it, fairly quickly.*)

LIZ. Just don't get too worked up about this. You don't need anything stressing you out right now.

(*LIZ heads back to the kitchen.*)

CHARLIE. I just want to make sure she's doing okay.

LIZ. She has a mother, Charlie. She's not alone, she has her mom.

CHARLIE. Well, she –

*(**CHARLIE** stops, choking on the meatball sub. **LIZ** remains in the kitchen, not noticing him.)*

*(Pause. **CHARLIE** starts to panic.)*

LIZ. What?

(no response)

Charlie, you okay?

*(**LIZ** comes out of the kitchen, sees **CHARLIE**.)*

LIZ. Oh God. Oh God, are you choking?! You're choking?!

*(**CHARLIE** leans forward as best he can, **LIZ** hits his back a few times. It doesn't help.)*

LIZ. Okay, okay – lean over the arm!

*(**CHARLIE** struggles to lean over the arm of the couch, stomach down. As best as she can, **LIZ** pushes on **CHARLIE**'s back, attempting the Heimlich Maneuver. Finally, she puts all her weight into it, and **CHARLIE** spits out the piece of food.)*

LIZ. *Shit.* Oh, shit, Charlie.

CHARLIE. *(breathing heavily)* I'm okay. I'm okay.

*(**LIZ** sits back down. **CHARLIE** rolls back into a sitting position on the couch. Long pause.)*

LIZ. GODDAMMIT CHARLIE, WHAT IS WRONG WITH YOU?

CHARLIE. I'm sorry –

LIZ. Chew your food like a normal human being! You could have choked to death just then, you realize that?! *You could have died right in front of me, you could have just – !*

*(Silence. **LIZ** breathes.)*

CHARLIE. I'm sorry, Liz.

*(Another silence. **LIZ** calms down. She looks at her watch, then grabs the remote control, turning on the television.)*

LIZ. *House* is on. Preview looked good, a guy whose arm has a mind of its own, something like that.

(pause)

You want a Dr. Pepper?

(pause)

CHARLIE. *(quiet)* I'm sorry, Liz.

LIZ. I asked if you want a Dr. Pepper.

(pause)

CHARLIE. *(quieter)* I'm sorry.

(Lights quickly snap to black.)

(The sound of waves returns, this time just a bit louder, rising in volume until lights rise on:)

WEDNESDAY

Morning.

(CHARLIE sits in front of the computer, as before, speaking into a microphone.)

CHARLIE. A lot of you had some questions about my most recent assignment, so I just wanted to clear up some misconceptions. This is a new teaching strategy I'm trying out, so please bear with me. First, when I asked you to "make it more personal", I was not being "creepy" as Tina436 recently commented. And when I asked you to "not edit your bad grammar or potentially subjective, unspecific, or just plain stupid ideas", I had not gone "apeshit insane yo" as UNCMark45 recently commented. Do you all realize that I can access the class discussion forum?

(pause)

Listen, at this point in this class, I've given you all I can in terms of structure, building athesis, paragraph organization. But for once – just write it. See what happens. It won't count toward your final grade, you can rewrite it later if you want, I just – I want to know what you really think. Okay?

Afternoon.

(**CHARLIE** *sits on the couch*, **ELLIE** *sits in a chair on the other side of the room, typing on her iPhone.*)

(**CHARLIE** *is reading an essay.*)

CHARLIE. This is…

(*pause*)

You say here that Walt Whitman wrote "Song *For* Myself".

ELLIE. (*not looking up*) Yeah?

CHARLIE. It's called "Song *of* Myself".

ELLIE. My title's better.

(*pause*)

CHARLIE. Yeah, well, it – … Okay, I'll just change it.

(**CHARLIE** *writes something in the essay. He keeps reading.*)

CHARLIE. Okay. "In the poem 'Song of Myself' by Walt Whitman, the author tells us how amazing he is. He tells us that he is better than everyone else, and that people should listen to what he says, because he is so wonderful."

ELLIE. You don't need to read it out loud. Just correct it.

CHARLIE. But it's not – … This really isn't what the poem is about.

ELLIE. Yes it is. I read it. It was really long and boring and it was about how great he thinks he is.

CHARLIE. But he's not really talking about himself, he's using the metaphor of "I" to refer to something a lot more universal. That's what's so amazing about the poem, on the surface it seems really self-involved and narcissistic, but actually it's about exploding the entire definition of the "self" in favor of this all-encompassing –

ELLIE. Oh my God I don't care.

(pause)

CHARLIE. You just want me to write it for you?

ELLIE. Yes.

CHARLIE. You don't want to understand the poem at all?

(ELLIE finally looks up from her iPhone.)

ELLIE. You think I don't understand it?

CHARLIE. Well –

ELLIE. You're just like my idiot teachers. You think because I don't go nuts over some stupid little poem, it's because I'm too stupid to understand it.

CHARLIE. I didn't say that –

ELLIE. Maybe I *do* understand it. Maybe I understand *exactly* what this poem is about, but I just don't care. Because it was written by some self-involved moron, and even though he thinks that his "metaphor for the self" is deep and shit, it doesn't mean anything because he's just some worthless nineteenth-century faggot. How about that?

(Pause. They stare at one another.)

CHARLIE. That's an interesting perspective.

ELLIE. You think you're funny?

CHARLIE. It could make for an interesting essay.

ELLIE. Oh my God shut up. Just fix it, okay? Write that thing about "exploding the definition of self", my English teacher will love that.

(ELLIE goes back to her iPhone. CHARLIE stares at her.)

CHARLIE. How's your mom doing?

ELLIE. Oh my God.

CHARLIE. I just thought we could – talk. A little.

ELLIE. If you're not going to write these essays for me, then I'm not gonna –

CHARLIE. Look, Ellie, I don't need you here to write this for you. I could write this essay in my sleep. And it's not fair of me to force you to stay here. If you really don't want to be here, you can go. You can still have the money.

(Pause. **ELLIE** *looks at* **CHARLIE**.)*

ELLIE. You'd let me have the money anyway?

CHARLIE. Yes.

ELLIE. I thought you wanted to get to know me.

CHARLIE. I do. But I don't want to force you to be here, that's not fair. It's up to you.

*(***ELLIE*** looks at him for a second, then puts away the iPhone.)*

ELLIE. She's fine. Mom. I guess.

CHARLIE. Have you told her that you're coming over here?

ELLIE. No. She'd be pretty angry. Plus, she'd want the money.

CHARLIE. Is she – happy?

ELLIE. When she drinks.

CHARLIE. Oh.

(pause)

Do you guys still live over in the duplex over on Orchard?

ELLIE. You don't even know where we live? How'd you get my cell-phone number?

CHARLIE. Facebook.

ELLIE. Creepy. You don't stay in touch with mom?

CHARLIE. Sometimes. She really only tells me things about you.

ELLIE. Why?

CHARLIE. Because that's all I ask about.

(pause)

ELLIE. When I was little we moved to an apartment on the other side of town, near the Circle K.

CHARLIE. Is your mother – with anyone now?

ELLIE. No. Why, you interested?

CHARLIE. Oh, no, I was just –

ELLIE. I'm kidding, Jesus. How could you be with anyone?

(*pause*)

Why did you gain all that weight?

CHARLIE. Oh, that doesn't –

ELLIE. If you're gonna interrogate me, I get to do the same thing. Why did you gain all that weight?

(*pause*)

CHARLIE. Someone very close to me passed away, and it – had an effect on me.

ELLIE. Who was it?

CHARLIE. My…

(**CHARLIE** *hesitates.*)

ELLIE. Your boyfriend?

CHARLIE. Yes, my boyfriend. My partner.

ELLIE. What was his name?

CHARLIE. Alan.

ELLIE. How'd he die?

CHARLIE. He sort of… Slowly killed himself.

(*pause*)

He had the flu, and it developed into pneumonia, but he got that sick because he – just sort of shut down. Stopped taking care of himself, stopped eating.

ELLIE. Why did he do that?

CHARLIE. He felt guilty.

(*quick pause*)

I'd rather not talk about this right now, is that alright with you?

ELLIE. Whatever.

(*pause*)

CHARLIE. I'll fix this essay for you before you leave, but I'd like you to do a little writing for me. Alright?

ELLIE. You were serious about that?

CHARLIE. Yes. Here.

> (**CHARLIE** *pulls out a notebook and a pen, hands them to* **ELLIE**.)

ELLIE. I hate writing essays.

CHARLIE. I know, just – be honest. Just think about the poem for a while, and write something. Write what you really think.

ELLIE. You want me to write what I really think?

CHARLIE. Yes. Don't worry about it being good, I'm the only person who will see it.

(short pause)

Okay, I'm going to be in the bathroom for a while, but I'll start working on your essay after –

ELLIE. I'm not helping you to the bathroom.

CHARLIE. I didn't ask you to help.

> (*With a lot of effort,* **CHARLIE** *manages to stand up with his walker. He makes his way to the bathroom.* **ELLIE** *starts writing absent-mindedly. After a sentence or so, she gets bored. She opens up* **CHARLIE***'s laptop and starts looking around.*)

> (*A knock at the door.*)

> (**ELLIE** *is about to call for* **CHARLIE***, then stops. She thinks for a moment.*)

> (**ELLIE** *goes to the door, opening it.* **ELDER THOMAS** *stands in the doorway.*)

ELDER THOMAS. Oh, hi – uh. I'm… I was looking for Charlie?

ELLIE. He's in the bathroom.

ELDER THOMAS. Oh, okay.

(short pause)

I can come back, if he –

ELLIE. No, it's fine. Come in.

(**ELDER THOMAS** *comes inside,* **ELLIE** *shuts the door behind him.*)

ELDER THOMAS. Are you his – friend?

ELLIE. I'm his daughter.

ELDER THOMAS. Oh. Wow, I... I didn't know that.

ELLIE. You surprised?

ELDER THOMAS. Yes.

ELLIE. What's more surprising? That a gay guy has a daughter, or that someone found his penis?

ELDER THOMAS. I really should go.

ELLIE. Don't be a pussy. That nametag makes you look like a retard.

ELDER THOMAS. We – have to wear them.

ELLIE. I don't care. What are you doing here again? Who are you?

ELDER THOMAS. Charlie said he – wanted to hear about the church. I'm with the Church of Jesus Christ of Latter Day Saints. I came by the other day, he wasn't feeling well, I thought I'd try him again. I brought some reading materials, and I thought we could talk about –

ELLIE. I'm bored.

ELDER THOMAS. Oh.

(*pause*)

ELLIE. I'll tell you one thing I like about religion. What I like about religion is that it assumes everyone is an idiot and that they're incapable of saving themselves. I think they got something right with that.

ELDER THOMAS. That's not really what I –

ELLIE. I'm not finished talking. I'm saying that I appreciate how religion makes people realize that, I appreciate that. But what I don't like about religion is that once people accept Jesus or whatever, they think they're more enlightened than everyone else. Like, by accepting the fact that they're stupid sinners, they've

become better than everyone else. And they turn into
assholes.

(pause)

ELDER THOMAS. I don't really know what to say. I have
some pamphlets –

ELLIE. Hold still.

ELDER THOMAS. What?

*(ELLIE takes out her iPhone, takes a picture of ELDER
THOMAS.)*

ELDER THOMAS. Why did you just do that?

ELLIE. Are you coming back tomorrow?

ELDER THOMAS. I don't – I'm not sure –

ELLIE. Come back tomorrow, I'll be here around the same
time.

ELDER THOMAS. I'm sorry, what's happening?

*(CHARLIE comes out of the bathroom with his walker,
sees ELDER THOMAS.)*

CHARLIE. Oh.

ELDER THOMAS. Hi, Charlie. I was just –

*(ELLIE takes a picture of CHARLIE, then puts the iPhone
back in her bag.)*

ELLIE. Will you have that done by tomorrow?

CHARLIE. Sure.

ELLIE. Five page minimum.

CHARLIE. I know. It'll be good, I promise.

(ELLIE extends a hand to ELDER THOMAS.)

ELLIE. I'm Ellie.

ELDER THOMAS. *(shaking her hand)* Elder Thomas.

ELLIE. Weird. See you later.

*(ELLIE exits. CHARLIE and ELDER THOMAS look at one
another.)*

ELDER THOMAS. Are you ready to hear about the Church?

(*pause*)

CHARLIE. Yes.

Later that Afternoon.

(CHARLIE sits in the same position as before, ELDER THOMAS holds some pamphlets. CHARLIE is glancing through one of them absentmindedly.)

ELDER THOMAS. It was written by prophets, pretty much in the same way that the Bible was written. Through revelation and prophecy by the Nephite prophet Mormon, who lived in the Americas in the fourth century. He transcribed the history of his people onto a set of golden plates, and then hundreds of years later Joseph Smith, a man from upstate New York, translated the book from the gold plates in about sixty-five days or so –

CHARLIE. You go to the church near the highway, right? The older one, the one by the U-haul?

ELDER THOMAS. Um – yeah. And to translate this book in sixty-five days is pretty remarkable because it means he had to translate the equivalent of about eight single-spaced pages per day –

CHARLIE. What's your name?

(pause)

ELDER THOMAS. I told you. It's Elder Thomas.

CHARLIE. But what's your real name?

ELDER THOMAS. Thomas.

CHARLIE. That's your last name, right? What's your first name?

ELDER THOMAS. You don't need to know my first name.

CHARLIE. Oh.

(pause)

ELDER THOMAS. What's also really incredible is that the Book of Mormon actually contains many distinct literary styles, including ancient Hebrew poetry and –

CHARLIE. Why is that incredible?

ELDER THOMAS. Well, it – how would some farm boy living in upstate New York have known how to write in the style of ancient Hebrew poetry? It's living proof of God's intervention.

CHARLIE. Hm.

(pause)

You know, actually – I know all this.

ELDER THOMAS. What do you mean?

CHARLIE. I've read just about every Wikipedia article about Mormonism –

ELDER THOMAS. I don't know if Wikipedia is the best source for –

CHARLIE. I also read the Book of Mormon.

ELDER THOMAS. The whole thing?

CHARLIE. Sure. A couple times.

(pause)

ELDER THOMAS. Did you – like it?

CHARLIE. I thought it was… Devastating.

ELDER THOMAS. Huh. Okay. I don't know about that.

CHARLIE. That one story about – Sherem? Sherem was questioning whether Jesus was actually God, so God struck Sherem down. And Sherem repented as he was dying, said that he was wrong, and so everyone believed in Jesus. God killed this man to – prove a point. That story, it's – devastating.

ELDER THOMAS. Yeah, that – I never thought about it like that, but –

(pause)

You know what I think is amazing? The Bible is great and everything, I mean – it's a really great way to come to understand God. But it's so – distant. This thing written thousands of years ago, on the other side of the planet, in languages we don't speak. It's been translated and translated, probably rewritten over and over and over. But the Book of Mormon – it's like, a direct link to God's word. One translator, writing in English, right here in America, just a few generations ago. It's –

CHARLIE. Devastating.

ELDER THOMAS. No. No, it's – hopeful. It makes you feel like there's some meaning to being here, right now, in America. Do you see that?

(pause)

You're so close in time and space to God's revelation, Charlie, that should make you feel proud. It should inspire you. It should keep you from doing this to yourself.

(pause)

CHARLIE. I'm not interested in converting, Elder Thomas. I don't find the Mormon Church hopeful. I don't find it amazing, and I don't find the proof convincing.

ELDER THOMAS. Wait so why did you want me to – ?

(pause)

Um. I want to just make sure that – . I want to make sure you know that I'm just coming over here to talk about the church. That's it.

CHARLIE. Well, yeah. What?

ELDER THOMAS. I just… I don't know if –

(pause, then suddenly)

You're not attracted to me, right?

CHARLIE. Oh my God.

ELDER THOMAS. It's just, with the – . What you were watching, the first time I came in here –

CHARLIE. I am not attracted to you. Please, understand me when I say that. *I am not attracted to you. You're a fetus.*

(pause)

Is that what you really think of me?

ELDER THOMAS. *No,* I –

CHARLIE. No, really. Tell me the truth. Do you find me disgusting?

(pause)

ELDER THOMAS. No.

(pause)

It's just that – you said you wanted to hear about the church.

CHARLIE. I did want to hear about the church. Your church, the one by the U-Haul, near the highway. I wanted to hear about *that* church.

ELDER THOMAS. I don't understand.

CHARLIE. You can go now, I'm sorry if I –

ELDER THOMAS. Is this about your – ? Your domestic – …

CHARLIE. How do you know about – ?

ELDER THOMAS. Your friend, Liz – she told me, she said that your – whatever, he had gone to the church?

CHARLIE. Look, you don't want to hear about this, you're just a kid –

ELDER THOMAS. I'm not a kid, I'm nineteen.

(pause)

Charlie – I've been going door to door for a while, you know? But no one understands that – I want to get to know them. The good and the bad, everything. How are we supposed to talk about your spiritual life if I don't know anything about who you are?

*(Pause. **CHARLIE** considers for a moment.)*

CHARLIE. His name – my partner's name, it was Alan.

(pause)

It sounds strange, but he was actually a student of mine. He was only a couple years younger than me, he had gone back to school after his mission. His parents were trying to get him to marry someone from the church, I think he barely knew her. But he was gonna go through with it – until he met me. It was ridiculous, he was the engaged son of a Mormon bishop, I had a wife and kid at home. But we just – couldn't stand to be apart.

(pause)

You really want me to keep going?

ELDER THOMAS. Yes. Really, yes.

CHARLIE. I thought he'd be able to get over all this religious stuff, but – ... It got worse and worse, to the point where every time we'd drive by that church near the highway he'd start to hyperventilate. His parents had abandoned him, refused to talk to him at all. But one night, about ten years ago, his father showed up here and told Alan he just wanted him to go to church the next day. He said, "I'm giving the talk tomorrow and I've written it for you. If you never come again – just come to church tomorrow." I told Alan not to go, but... The next morning he came home afterward, and he was just – hollow. It took him over, and he just – stopped everything. He stopped bathing, he stopped eating, he stopped sleeping. And a few months later, he was gone.

ELDER THOMAS. What happened? At the service?

CHARLIE. I don't know. Alan wouldn't tell me what they did to him. I guess – I was hoping you could find out.

(pause)

ELDER THOMAS. I don't – I'm not even from here, I don't know if –

CHARLIE. I know – nevermind. It's ridiculous.

(pause)

ELDER THOMAS. I'm going to ask around, alright? I'll see if anyone remembers that day, the last day he was there. Who knows, someone might remember.

CHARLIE. You'd do that?

ELDER THOMAS. Of course. I just want to help. That's why I'm on a mission in the first place, right?

*(**LIZ** enters through the door with an extra wide wheelchair and a shopping bag.)*

LIZ. Alright, I got you something. I did some asking around, and this doctor said –

*(**LIZ** notices **ELDER THOMAS**.)*

LIZ. What the hell, Charlie?

ELDER THOMAS. I was just –

LIZ. *Charlie?*

CHARLIE. It's fine, Liz.

LIZ. What did I say about your stress level? You don't need someone coming over and telling you that you're going to hell.

ELDER THOMAS. I never said that, I would never say that.

LIZ. Leave.

CHARLIE. Liz –

LIZ. *Get out.*

ELDER THOMAS. Okay.

*(**ELDER THOMAS** heads for the door.)*

CHARLIE. Liz, stop it. He didn't do anything to you, for Christ's sake. He's just a kid.

ELDER THOMAS. I'm nineteen.

(pause)

I'll just go –

LIZ. Actually – stay. We'll have a chat.

*(to **CHARLIE**)*

I brought you this.

CHARLIE. Thank you. What is it?

LIZ. What the fuck does it look like? It's a fat guy wheelchair.

CHARLIE. Why do I need a wheelchair?

LIZ. I was talking to one of the E.R. doctors, he told me that moderate activity would be a good idea. That a sense of independence would help you keep your spirits up. Now you don't have to sit on that couch all day long.

CHARLIE. How much did you pay for this thing?

LIZ. Nothing. We ordered it specially for a patient a few months ago, it's just been sitting around.

CHARLIE. What happened to the patient?

LIZ. Try it out. Now you can go to the bedroom by yourself, get to the bathroom more easily.

*(**LIZ** moves the wheelchair next to **CHARLIE**.)*

*(**CHARLIE** braces himself on his walker and manages to pull himself up.)*

*(**LIZ** positions the wheelchair behind **CHARLIE**, **CHARLIE** starts slowly backing into the wheelchair.)*

LIZ. *(cont.) (ala a truck backing up)* Beep. Beep. Beep. Beep.

*(**CHARLIE** stops, looks back at her. **LIZ** smiles.)*

*(**CHARLIE** continues, then sits in the wheelchair, wheezing loudly. He tries it out, wheeling himself a few feet.)*

Good?

CHARLIE. Yeah, it's – . It's actually nice.

(rolls a few more feet)

Thank you, Liz, it's really –

LIZ. Why don't you see if it fits through the bedroom door, you probably haven't been in there for days, right?

ELDER THOMAS. I should probably go –

LIZ. Not before we have our little chat.

ELDER THOMAS. Oh, I. What?

CHARLIE. Liz –

LIZ. *(to **CHARLIE**)* Give us a few minutes.

*(**LIZ** pushes him toward the bedroom, out of the room. **LIZ** turns back to **ELDER THOMAS**, stares at him.)*

Take a seat.

*(**ELDER THOMAS** sits down.)*

So. Iowa?

ELDER THOMAS. What?

LIZ. You're from Iowa.

ELDER THOMAS. Uh. Yes.

LIZ. What part?

ELDER THOMAS. Waterloo?

LIZ. You asking me?

ELDER THOMAS. No, I – I'm from Waterloo.

(*Pause.* **LIZ** *smokes.*)

LIZ. So listen. You're just a kid, you don't know anything. But I want to be very clear with you about a few things if you're going to keep coming over here.

(*pause*)

I know this is fun for you. You get to travel around, act superior to everyone else. Plus you get to go home, get married, get some boring job, have tons of kids, and when you die you get your own planet. It all sounds pretty awesome. But, there are other kinds of people. People like Charlie, for whom this amazing plan doesn't fit. You can't fit a round peg in a square hole, and you certainly can't fit a morbidly obese gay peg in a Mormon hole. That came out wrong.

(*pause*)

Point is – you're a sweet kid, but he doesn't need this right now.

ELDER THOMAS. I disagree.

(*pause*)

LIZ. Excuse me?

ELDER THOMAS. Sorry, I just – I think this is exactly what he needs right now. He's refusing to go to the hospital, he's dying – what he needs is some spiritual guidance.

LIZ. And you're gonna give him that?

ELDER THOMAS. No. God will.

LIZ. I see.

(*pause*)

My big brother went on a mission. Went to Switzerland.

ELDER THOMAS. Oh.

LIZ. Yeah. He was the good kid. I however was the black sheep – by the time I was thirteen, I refused to go to church, told my dad I didn't believe in God. Even had to move out of the house, went to live with my aunt and uncle in Boise until I graduated. But not my big brother – he was a good Mormon. He wrote me a letter a few months into his mission, he told me he was cold all the time. That he was cold all the time, and lonely, but he preferred being out there in Switzerland because he didn't want to come back and get married.

ELDER THOMAS. He didn't want to – ?

LIZ. Dad had set it all up, pushed him into getting engaged to this girl from the church he barely knew. When he came back, he refused to go through with the wedding. Fell in love with someone else, started a whole new life. Until one day, when he went back to the church – I don't know what the hell they did to him that day, but it sure fucked him up. And after that he just started wasting away until he was just – gone.

(pause)

That was my brother. Alan. My big brother who was *crushed* under the church that you think can save Charlie.

ELDER THOMAS. Oh.

*(Silence. **LIZ** stares at him, smoking.)*

ELDER THOMAS. I'm sorry.

LIZ. What the fuck are you sorry about?

(pause)

Where's your companion?

ELDER THOMAS. What?

LIZ. You always have to be in pairs. I know that. It's sort of a big deal for you to be out here alone, isn't it?

(pause)

ELDER THOMAS. Elder Johnson. He's – not feeling well.

LIZ. Not feeling well?

ELDER THOMAS. Why does it matter?

LIZ. It's a pretty big deal for you guys not to –

ELDER THOMAS. Well, to be honest, he's having some – problems and he's pretty useless right now, but I thought I could do some good. By myself. Help just *one* person.

LIZ. And that one person is Charlie.

ELDER THOMAS. Yes.

(**CHARLIE** *comes out of the bedroom.* **LIZ** *doesn't notice him.*)

LIZ. Listen to me. He doesn't need your help, he doesn't want saving. In a few days he's probably going to be dead, and right now what he needs is for you to leave him alone. I am the only person who knows how to take care of him, do you understand? *I am the only one who can save him.*

CHARLIE. Liz.

(**LIZ** *turns around, sees* **CHARLIE**. **ELDER THOMAS** *quickly gathers his things and exits.* **LIZ** *forces a smile.*)

LIZ. Everything go alright in there?

(no response)

I've got an hour or so before I need to get back, we could watch some Maury. Wheel yourself over here, c'mon.

(**LIZ** *turns on the television.* **CHARLIE** *stares at her, not moving.*)

Night.

(**CHARLIE**, *alone, in his wheelchair. He is laying some blankets out for the night onto the couch. After a moment, he notices* **ELLIE**'s *notebook. He wheels himself over to it, picks it up, opens it.*)

CHARLIE. *(reading)* "This apartment smells. This notebook is retarded. I hate everyone."

(**CHARLIE** *looks at it for a moment, smiling.*)

CHARLIE. "This apartment smells. This notebook is retarded. I hate everyone."

(**CHARLIE** *laughs a little. The laugh quickly turns into a cough, which produces pain in his chest. He takes a few breaths, trying to calm himself down.*)

CHARLIE. *(soft)* I felt saddest of all when I read the boring chapters that were only descriptions of whales, because I knew that the author was just trying to save us from his own sad story, just for a little while. This apartment smells.

(**CHARLIE** *takes a few deep breaths, wheezing. The pain starts to subside.*)

CHARLIE. This apartment smells. This notebook is retarded. I hate everyone. The author was just trying to save us from his own sad story, just for a little while. I hate everyone. The author was just trying to –

(Lights quickly snap to black.)

(In the darkness, once again we hear the sound of waves – louder now, and more distinct, building a little in volume before lights rise on:)

THURSDAY

Morning.

(CHARLIE sits on the wheelchair, in front of his laptop, speaking into the microphone.)

CHARLIE. KimmyBallz429, I read your recent post on the discussion forum about strategies for coming up with a good thesis. You said that I want you to "just pick a sentence from the book and say it's good or some shit".

(pause)

I think I owe you all an apology. I've been teaching you all to rewrite and rewrite and rewrite, to edit your thoughts and change them and make them clearer, more precise, more objective. And I'm starting to realize that that's horseshit. You don't have any true reaction to these books because I've taught you to edit your reactions, to reshape them and reconfigure them over and over. And after all that, you don't even have a reaction at all. You just end up hating it.

(pause)

How about this? Don't write about the book. Forget the assignment, forget the readings. Hell, forget everything you know about what makes a good essay and just – write. Just sit down, and write me something. Just give me something honest. Okay?

Later that Morning.

(**ELLIE** *stands by the door, holding an essay.*)

ELLIE. So it's good?

CHARLIE. It's really, really good.

ELLIE. What grade am I gonna get?

CHARLIE. It's a really good essay.

ELLIE. Yeah, whatever. Okay bye.

(**ELLIE** *turns to the door.*)

CHARLIE. I was hoping you could write a little more in your notebook.

ELLIE. Oh my God.

CHARLIE. You've only written a couple sentences so far – could you write me some more?

ELLIE. I kind of hate you.

CHARLIE. Yeah, but you hate everyone.

(*pause*)

Look, just keep going with what you were doing. Forget the poem, forget about writing an essay. Just keep going, write about whatever you want, whatever you're thinking –

ELLIE. Shut up, just give me the notebook.

(**CHARLIE** *hands* **ELLIE** *the notebook, she sits down, opens the notebook. She is about to write, then looks at* **CHARLIE**.)

ELLIE. My mom found out. That I'm coming here.

(*pause*)

CHARLIE. How?

ELLIE. Small town bullshit. Her friend Judy saw the car parked outside here.

(*pause*)

She asked me how big you were.

CHARLIE. She knows that I – ?

ELLIE. She just heard you gained weight. She doesn't know you're a monster.

(pause)

She made me promise to stop coming over.

CHARLIE. Did you tell her about the money?

ELLIE. I'm not retarded.

(Pause. **ELLIE** *writes a bit,* **CHARLIE** *watches her.)*

CHARLIE. I was in a strange place in my life when I married your mom.

ELLIE. Did I fucking ask?

CHARLIE. Sorry. I just thought you… I'm sure your mom has told you the whole story anyway.

ELLIE. No, she hasn't, she doesn't like talking about you. Ever. But I'm pretty sure I know the story anyway. You come home one day, "Oh, honey, I'm so repressed, I need to self-actualize or some stupid shit." And mom starts screaming, then you're on the floor, just like I remember, looking pathetic and fat. Is that it?

(pause)

CHARLIE. I understand that you're angry.

ELLIE. Oh my God.

CHARLIE. But you don't need to be angry at the entire world. I'm the asshole, just be angry at me, don't take it out on –

ELLIE. You think you're the only person who's ever fucked me over? Trust me, I have a list. And you're no more important than any other asshole that's treated me like dirt.

*(***ELLIE*** *goes back to writing.* **CHARLIE** *watches her. A few moments pass.)*

ELLIE. You could have sent her money, you know.

CHARLIE. What?

ELLIE. If you have all that money. You could have been sending money to my mom.

CHARLIE. I did.

ELLIE. I mean more than just child support.

(long silence)

CHARLIE. I did.

(pause)

I'm so sorry, Ellie. I'm so, so sorry.

(ELLIE *looks up from her notebook for a second, then goes back to writing. A few moments pass.* **ELLIE** *puts the pen down, looks at* **CHARLIE.** *)*

ELLIE. I'm hungry.

(pause)

CHARLIE. There's stuff for sandwiches in the kitchen.

ELLIE. Okay.

(pause)

I'll make you one, but it's going to be small. And I'm only using turkey or chicken, and no mayonnaise.

(pause)

CHARLIE. Thank you.

(ELLIE *gets up, moves toward the kitchen.)*

CHARLIE. What were you writing about?

ELLIE. I was writing about how when you die, you won't fit through the door or the windows. So they'll probably have to take you out in pieces.

(ELLIE *exits into the kitchen.)*

Afternoon.

(CHARLIE is asleep in his wheelchair. ELLIE is sitting on the couch typing on CHARLIE's laptop, smoking pot from a small glass pipe.)

(a knock at the door)

(ELLIE puts the pipe in CHARLIE's hand. CHARLIE doesn't wake up.)

ELLIE. Yeah?

ELDER THOMAS. *(from outside)* I, uh – hello?

(ELLIE pauses for a second, recognizing the voice, then takes the pipe out of CHARLIE's hand. She goes to the door, opening it. ELDER THOMAS stands in the doorway holding his bicycle helmet.)

ELLIE. What?

ELDER THOMAS. Oh, I –

ELLIE. What?

ELDER THOMAS. Hi.

(sees the pipe)

Are you – ?

ELLIE. I'm bored. Come inside.

ELDER THOMAS. Maybe I should –

ELLIE. Oh my God stop talking. Take that nametag off, I told you, you look like a retard.

(ELLIE closes the door behind ELDER THOMAS.)

ELDER THOMAS. *(seeing CHARLIE)* Is he… ?

ELLIE. Do you ever finish sentences? He's asleep.

ELDER THOMAS. I can come back.

ELLIE. He'll be asleep for a while.

ELDER THOMAS. Oh. Is he okay?

ELLIE. I don't know. I ground up some Ambien and put it in his sandwich.

ELDER THOMAS. Oh my God, is he – ?

ELLIE. I only gave him a couple, he's fine. I can take three at a time.

ELDER THOMAS. Why did you – ? You have Ambien? Where did you get Ambien?

ELLIE. I had sex with a pharmacist. Just kidding, gross. My mom eats them like tic tacs. Do you ever wear anything different?

ELDER THOMAS. Should he be taking sleeping pills? He's sort of sick and –

ELLIE. Yeah, anyway. Why is your name "Elder"?

ELDER THOMAS. It's not my real… During the mission, we all get called "Elder". My last name is Thomas, so – I'm Elder Thomas.

ELLIE. It makes you sound, like, important. Which you're not.

(**ELLIE** *takes a hit from the pipe.* **ELDER THOMAS** *watches.*)

ELDER THOMAS. No, I'm not.

ELLIE. Does this make you nervous?

ELDER THOMAS. No, I – . Well, yeah, it does.

ELLIE. It's just pot, it's not like I'm smoking crack or anything. You probably have no idea what I'm talking about.

ELDER THOMAS. Don't – . I know what you're talking about. I know what drugs are.

ELLIE. You only think you know what drugs are because your parents told you a whole bunch of lies about them. You probably think that smoking pot will turn you into a homeless person or something.

ELDER THOMAS. You know, I'm not an idiot. I've smoked pot before.

ELLIE. Oo, I'm so impressed.

ELDER THOMAS. I'm not trying to impress you, I'm just saying –

ELLIE. You have not smoked pot.

ELDER THOMAS. Yes, I have. It was – kind of a problem.

ELLIE. A "problem"?

ELDER THOMAS. My bishop told me I had an addiction.

ELLIE. That is the stupidest fucking thing I have ever heard in my entire life.

(**ELLIE** *takes a hit, holds it in.*)

ELDER THOMAS. I was doing it every day. I had a problem.

ELLIE. You were a stoner. You had a hobby.

(**ELLIE** *exhales, blowing the hit in* **ELDER THOMAS**' *face.*)

ELDER THOMAS. Okay, I'm leaving.

(**ELDER THOMAS** *gets up.*)

ELLIE. If you leave, I'll feed him the rest of the pills I have in the bottle.

(**ELDER THOMAS** *stops.*)

ELDER THOMAS. What?

ELLIE. There's probably twenty or thirty more. I'll crush them up and mix them into some water and pour it down his throat.

ELDER THOMAS. Why would you say something like that?

ELLIE. Sit down.

ELDER THOMAS. You wouldn't really do that, would you?

ELLIE. Oh my God sit down.

(**ELDER THOMAS** *pauses, then comes back to the couch and sits down.*)

ELLIE. Why do you keep coming back here?

ELDER THOMAS. He wants me to come over, he told me. He needs help.

ELLIE. That's a stupid reason. Take a hit.

ELDER THOMAS. What? No.

ELLIE. You've never smoked before.

ELDER THOMAS. Yes, I have.

ELLIE. You're some sheltered little Mormon boy, you haven't done anything. You don't know anything. God, I can't even look at you.

ELDER THOMAS. Why do you talk like that, is this how you treat everyone?

ELLIE. Yeah. Why does he want to talk to you?

ELDER THOMAS. I think he needs God to be in his life right now.

ELLIE. That's an even stupider reason. Do you think he wants to have sex with you? That's so gross, oh my God. Take a hit.

ELDER THOMAS. He doesn't want to – ! I don't want to take a hit!

ELLIE. Why are you such a *pussy?* You wear a *bicycle helmet.* Take a hit.

(ELLIE *shoves the pipe into* ELDER THOMAS' *chest.*)

ELDER THOMAS. I told you –

ELLIE. If you don't take a hit, I'm going to call the police and tell them you tried to rape me. Take a hit.

(*pause*)

ELDER THOMAS. I don't understand you at all.

ELLIE. Oh my God.

(ELDER THOMAS *takes the pipe.*)

ELDER THOMAS. Is there a carb on this?

ELLIE. Oo, I'm so impressed.

ELDER THOMAS. I wasn't trying to –

ELLIE. There isn't a carb.

(ELDER THOMAS *takes a hit. He exhales.*)

(ELLIE *takes out her iPhone and snaps a quick picture* ELDER THOMAS *as he exhales.*)

ELDER THOMAS. (*coughing*) What are you doing? Why did you just – ?

ELLIE. Calm down. Take another hit.

ELDER THOMAS. What are you going to do with that picture?

ELLIE. I'm gonna masturbate to it, is that what you want me to say? You're a pervert. Take another hit.

*(No response. **ELDER THOMAS** stares at her.)*

ELLIE. Look, I'm just fucking with you, alright? I'm not gonna kill anyone, I'm not gonna tell anyone you raped me. I don't understand why people believe everything I say. People are such idiots, it's so easy, it's ridiculous.

ELDER THOMAS. You aren't going to feed him more Ambien?

ELLIE. No.

ELDER THOMAS. Did you really put some in his sandwich?

ELLIE. That I did. Just a couple. So he'd stop bugging me.

ELDER THOMAS. Why don't you just leave?

ELLIE. I don't know.

ELDER THOMAS. If you hate him so much why do you keep coming over?

ELLIE. I'm done answering questions now.

ELDER THOMAS. Okay.

(silence)

Can I have another hit?

ELLIE. It goes against your religion, and that makes you a hypocrite. Go ahead.

*(**ELDER THOMAS** takes another hit – a big one.)*

ELDER THOMAS. I never really thought I had a problem. I did it every day for a while, then I stopped. If I was able to stop then how is it a problem?

ELLIE. That's the only smart thing you've said since you came in here.

ELDER THOMAS. This is really good weed.

ELLIE. No it's not. You just haven't smoked in a while.

*(**ELLIE** takes another picture of him.)*

ELDER THOMAS. I really wish you wouldn't do that.

ELLIE. Yeah, I heard you the first time. Do you find me attractive?

ELDER THOMAS. I –

ELLIE. Because I'm not attracted to you at all, just to let you know.

(pause)

ELDER THOMAS. Okay.

ELLIE. I'm not trying to be mean or anything. But I just don't think you're good looking or interesting. Or intelligent.

ELDER THOMAS. *(a little hurt)* Oh.

ELLIE. Oh my God grow up. Maybe someone else finds you attractive, just not me. Maybe my dad finds you attractive.

ELDER THOMAS. I really wish you wouldn't say that.

ELLIE. It's so easy to make you uncomfortable, it's a little sad. You can cash that out.

ELDER THOMAS. You don't mind?

ELLIE. No.

*(**ELDER THOMAS** takes another big hit from the pipe. He's pretty high by this point.)*

ELDER THOMAS. I don't know if I'm going to be able to bike back to my apartment.

ELLIE. Wow, you're pretty high, aren't you?

ELDER THOMAS. Yes. Yes, I am. And if my parents knew I was getting high, that I was getting high while I was on my *mission* –

ELLIE. You're not on a mission.

(pause)

ELDER THOMAS. What?

ELLIE. I said you're not on a mission. Jesus.

(*pause*)

I remembered your name from your name-tag. The Mormon website has a search engine for, like, everything. Anyway, there was a list of twelve people on missions in northern Idaho, and you're not one of them.

(*pause*)

ELDER THOMAS. They didn't update the website.

ELLIE. I'm not a retard.

(*pause*)

ELDER THOMAS. I need to go.

ELLIE. You keep saying that. Why are you pretending to be a Mormon missionary?

ELDER THOMAS. I'm not – I *am* on a mission –

ELLIE. Oh my God.

ELDER THOMAS. I mean I – *was*. I was on a mission.

ELLIE. Here?

ELDER THOMAS. I have to go.

(**ELDER THOMAS** *stands up, a little shaky on his feet.*)

ELLIE. What happened?

ELDER THOMAS. *Why do you care?!*

ELLIE. Because I think we have a blossoming friendship.

(*Pause.* **ELDER THOMAS** *looks at her.*)

ELDER THOMAS. I thought you said I wasn't attractive or interesting or intelligent.

ELLIE. So?

ELDER THOMAS. So why would you want to be my friend?

ELLIE. Because everyone else I know is even less attractive, interesting, and intelligent than you.

(*pause*)

ELDER THOMAS. You won't tell anyone?

ELLIE. Who am I gonna tell?

> *(Pause.* **ELDER THOMAS** *goes back to the couch, sitting next to* **ELLIE.***)*

ELDER THOMAS. I was in Eastern Oregon, in Pendleton. It's where they do that big annual rodeo, the famous one –

ELLIE. I really, really don't care about that.

ELDER THOMAS. Anyway, I was on my mission there. Last year.

ELLIE. What happened?

ELDER THOMAS. I left. I didn't want to do it anymore.

> *(pause)*

> We just kept trying to talk to people, really *engage* with them, but most of the time they'd just talk to us for a little while, say "thank you", and we'd never hear from them again. So after a while, it was like – what am I *actually doing* here? Am I really, like, really *helping* people?

ELLIE. No you were not.

ELDER THOMAS. I started to feel that way, too.

ELLIE. I don't *feel* that way, I *know* that you weren't helping people. Like, for a fact. It doesn't help people to tell them how to believe in God. Why would that help people?

ELDER THOMAS. It might bring them eternal salvation.

ELLIE. Oh my God you actually think that?

ELDER THOMAS. Yeah… Maybe.

ELLIE. "Maybe"? You're shitty at being a religious person.

ELDER THOMAS. I just – I *want* to believe it. My family, all my friends, they seem like – totally happy. I wanna be like that.

ELLIE. So why did you come to Idaho?

ELDER THOMAS. I got kicked off the mission.

ELLIE. For smoking pot?

ELDER THOMAS. For assaulting my companion.

(*pause*)

ELLIE. You're full of shit.

ELDER THOMAS. No, I'm not.

ELLIE. Oh my God you so are.

ELDER THOMAS. Seriously.

ELLIE. So what, like, you went on a "pot bender"?

ELDER THOMAS. I wasn't smoking at all. The moment I stepped foot in Oregon, I made a promise to myself that I wouldn't smoke any more. And I didn't.

ELLIE. Which is a shame if it's your first time in Oregon. So why did you beat him up?

ELDER THOMAS. He just... He didn't care. About anything. We'd go out every day, we'd try to talk to people, and no one would listen, and he *didn't even care*. I tried to talk to him about different sections of town we could go to, different ways to engage them, different ways to *help* these people... But you could tell, if we spent our whole mission there ministering and hadn't helped *one single person*, he wouldn't have cared. His faith was just – . He didn't need to earn it or prove it *at all*. And one day, we were out in this little farming community, and we weren't helping anyone, and he kept complaining about being hungry, and how hot it was out that day, and – I just lost it. I went nuts.

(*pause*)

He told me his parents would sue me, that I'd go to jail. All I wanted to do was finish this mission, I wanted to see Mormonism help *one person*. So, I just got on a bus. I still have a few thousand dollars left in my checking account. I went to the church here in town a couple times, I found this nametag in the common room.

ELLIE. You have like *huge* pores on your face, did you know you have huge pores?

ELDER THOMAS. Were you listening to me? Why did you just say that?

ELLIE. So what's your real name?

ELDER THOMAS. Why do you want to know?

ELLIE. Because we're friends now.

(*pause*)

ELDER THOMAS. Joseph Paulson.

(**ELLIE** *takes a picture of him.*)

ELLIE. You're slightly more interesting now.

ELDER THOMAS. Thank you.

(*The door bursts open revealing* **MARY**, *a woman of about forty but who looks considerably older.*)

ELLIE. Shit.

(**MARY** *pushes past* **ELLIE**, *sees* **CHARLIE**. *She stops immediately. Long silence as she stares at* **CHARLIE**. *She moves toward him slowly.*)

ELLIE. Mom –

MARY. Shut up.

(*She stands next to* **CHARLIE**, *looking down at him.*)

MARY. Charlie.

(**CHARLIE** *doesn't move.*)

MARY. *Charlie.*

(*No response.* **MARY** *looks at* **ELLIE**. **ELLIE** *looks away.*)

ELLIE. Yeah okay sorry.

Late Afternoon.

(CHARLIE sits in his wheelchair, awake but very groggy. LIZ is attaching an oxygen tank to the wheelchair, running a tube over his ears and under his nose. MARY sits on the couch smoking a cigarette. ELLIE stands by the door, ELDER THOMAS in the opposite corner.)

(Throughout the scene, CHARLIE's breathing is much more shallow, and his wheezing is much worse.)

LIZ. *(to MARY)* You know, he's not breathing so good. Second-hand smoke isn't really a great idea.

CHARLIE. She's fine, Liz.

LIZ. What, are you a doctor?

MARY. No, and neither are you.

(MARY puts out the cigarette in an empty soda can.)

(MARY stares at CHARLIE.)

LIZ. Are you having more pain?

CHARLIE. Yes. Wheezing's getting worse.

LIZ. How easy is it to move?

CHARLIE. Not very.

LIZ. How about any confusion? Have you felt disoriented, confused, forgotten where you are or what you're doing?

CHARLIE. No. Would that be bad?

LIZ. Yes. That would be very bad.

CHARLIE. So – am I okay?

LIZ. No, you're not "okay". But as far as the sleeping pills, you're fine. I think she only gave you a couple.

ELLIE. Yeah, that's what I told you.

(LIZ takes off the stethoscope, moves toward ELLIE.)

LIZ. Listen to me. I was a very angry, very stupid little girl once too, but this goes beyond smoking pot and posting shit on the internet. If you would have given him more pills than that, you could have –

ELLIE. Yeah, except I didn't give him more than that, I gave him *two pills.*

MARY. *(to* **ELLIE***)* Ellie, how much money did he offer you?

CHARLIE. Mary. Don't.

MARY. *(to* **CHARLIE***)* All of it? It would have to be all of it. It would take quite a lot of money to make that girl do something she doesn't want to do.

ELLIE. How do you know about – ?

MARY. *(to* **ELLIE***)* You think I'm an idiot? You think for one second I would believe that you were coming here out of the kindness of your heart?

ELLIE. You're not getting any of it. He said I could have all of it.

LIZ. Charlie doesn't have any money. I do all his shopping, I know exactly how much is in his checking account.

(Pause.)

MARY. *(to* **CHARLIE***)* She doesn't know?

CHARLIE. Mary –

MARY. *(to* **LIZ***)* Where do you think all the money from his teaching has been going? The account for Ellie – by now it has to be huge.

(to **CHARLIE***)*

Over a hundred thousand at least, right?

LIZ. *(to* **CHARLIE***)* That isn't true, is it?

(pause)

Charlie, we could have gotten you anything you needed – special beds, physical therapists, fucking *health insurance* – ... Last year when my car broke down, and I had to walk through the snow to get your groceries –

CHARLIE. I offered to get your car fixed –

LIZ. And I refused because I thought you had seven hundred dollars in your bank account.

(pause)

You had all that money that you were keeping a *secret* from me? Why were you doing that? What, you think I would try and *take* it from you?

CHARLIE. No, of course not, I… It's for Ellie. It's always been for Ellie.

(pause)

If there was ever some kind of emergency, I would have given you money –

LIZ. Would you? You've been keeping this from me for years, you really think I can trust you?

(Pause. LIZ starts grabbing her things.)

CHARLIE. Please don't go.

(LIZ exits. Pause.)

ELLIE. Mom – you're not getting any of my money.

MARY. Oh, shut up, Ellie.

(pause)

Both of you, leave. Right now.

(pause)

ELLIE. I need the car keys.

MARY. You can walk.

ELLIE. It's like two miles!

MARY. Do you really think that I care?

ELLIE. I hate you.

(ELLIE exits. ELDER THOMAS moves out of the corner, moving toward CHARLIE.)

ELDER THOMAS. I'll come back.

(CHARLIE looks at him.)

(ELDER THOMAS exits. A long moment of silence.)

(MARY stares at CHARLIE. She stands up, still looking at him. She circles his wheelchair, looking at him from all sides.)

MARY. Jesus, Charlie.

*(Pause. **MARY** looks away. She takes a cigarette out of her purse, lights it up.)*

MARY. So this – heart thing. It's serious, yeah?

CHARLIE. Pretty serious.

MARY. You gonna be okay?

(pause)

CHARLIE. I'll be fine.

(pause)

MARY. Do you have anything?

CHARLIE. What?

(pause)

Oh, uh – maybe, in the kitchen. There might be something in the cabinet over the stove, the highest shelf on the right.

*(**MARY** goes to the kitchen, retrieves a bottle of vodka and a glass. She pours a large drink for herself, drinks.)*

MARY. Our deal was we'd wait until she was out of the house to give her the money.

CHARLIE. What's the difference?

MARY. The difference is she's seventeen and in high school. She's going to spend it on ponies or marijuana or something.

CHARLIE. I think she's a little smarter than that.

MARY. I really wish you wouldn't have done this, Charlie. This is the last thing I need right now.

(taking a long drink)

How has it been? Getting to know her.

CHARLIE. She's – amazing.

*(**MARY** chuckles.)*

MARY. You still do that.

CHARLIE. What?

MARY. That positivity. It's so annoying.

CHARLIE. *(smiling)* Well, you're a complete cynic, I was just trying to balance us out.

MARY. I guess I do miss that. That one thing.

CHARLIE. Just that?

MARY. That, and the cooking. Last month I tried to make a pie and I nearly set the entire apartment building on fire, Ellie threw all our pots and pans into the dumpster so I'd never try to do it again. You still cook?

CHARLIE. Not for years now. It's – hard for me to get into the kitchen.

(pause)

MARY. Charlie, I… I never knew you were doing this to yourself.

CHARLIE. You never asked me how I was doing.

MARY. You never asked me how I was doing either. Every month it's just, "how much money do you need?" and "how's Ellie?"

CHARLIE. You didn't tell me she was failing out of high school.

MARY. Well, now you know. I guess I just didn't need the lecture from you about my involvement in her education.

CHARLIE. That's not what I –

(long pause)

How are you doing, Mary?

(pause)

MARY. Fine.

CHARLIE. Are you working?

MARY. No.

CHARLIE. Do you need me to send more money?

MARY. *No.*

(pause)

CHARLIE. It's good to see you.

(pause)

Mary, I know that I screwed everything up. I know it must have been terrible. And humiliating. And I know that I'm not supposed to be around her – hell, you could call the police if you want to –

MARY. Christ, you really think I'd do that?

CHARLIE. You fought me pretty hard for full custody. And I don't blame you, after what I did. But I just want to see her – I've *always* just wanted to see her. Is it so awful that she has a gay father?

MARY. No, actually, it's not.

(pause)

She's – awful, isn't she?

CHARLIE. What?

MARY. Ellie. She's awful. She's a terror.

CHARLIE. No, she's – she has a strong personality, but –

MARY. Charlie, she doesn't even have any *friends*. Not a single one. She's so cruel that no one at school will even *talk* to her.

(pause)

When she was nine, ten, I thought – I'm not giving him the satisfaction. I'm not letting him see this awful little girl and blame it all on me. No way.

CHARLIE. Wait, is that why you've been keeping her from me all this time? You thought I would think you were a bad mother?

MARY. At first. But later on – when she was fifteen, sixteen. I was worried she would hurt you.

CHARLIE. "Hurt" me? That's ridiculous –

MARY. You've been around her for two days now, and already she's almost killed you.

(pause)

I was protecting you, Charlie. You've always been so fucking sensitive, ready to break down over anything… And here's this girl – this girl who takes *pleasure* in hurting people, this *terrible* girl.

(pause)

Believe me Charlie, I don't take any pleasure in admitting it, I'm her mother for Christ's sake. I spent way too many years saying to myself, she's just rebellious, she's just difficult. Charlie – she's evil.

CHARLIE. She is not evil.

(Pause. **MARY** *goes to* **CHARLIE***'s laptop, types.)*

CHARLIE. What are you doing?

MARY. Just – .

CHARLIE. If you're gonna show me Ellie's site, I've already seen it –

MARY. Did you see what she posted this morning?

*(***MARY*** brings the computer to* **CHARLIE***.)*

*(***CHARLIE*** looks at the screen.)*

MARY. When I saw this picture of you… I thought I should come over.

*(***CHARLIE*** continues looking at the computer.)*

CHARLIE. *(reading)* "There'll be a grease fire in Hell when he starts to burn."

(pause)

MARY. Don't feel bad, I've made quite a few appearances on that little site of hers.

(pause)

You okay?

(pause)

CHARLIE. She's a strong writer.

MARY. *That's* your response?

CHARLIE. This isn't evil, this is honesty. Do you know how much bullshit I've read in my life?

MARY. My God, things never change. I don't understand you, Charlie.

CHARLIE. Every time I called you, I'd ask about her and you'd tell me she was doing fine. If she's so evil, why didn't you ever –

MARY. What was I supposed to tell you? That she was off treating her friends like dirt and slashing her teachers' tires? You didn't want to hear about that stuff.

CHARLIE. I could have helped her!

MARY. She doesn't want your help! She doesn't want anyone!

(**MARY** *gets up, wandering aimlessly around the room, drunk by this point and a little shaky on her feet.*)

CHARLIE. Mary, sit down.

MARY. You think I didn't want her to have a dad? She *adored* you. The only reason you married me in the first place was to have a kid, I know that.

CHARLIE. *Mary. Please.*

(**MARY** *stops, gets her drink and sits back down.*)

MARY. This brings back memories, doesn't it?

(*pause*)

Listen. I... I never got to say that I was sorry.

CHARLIE. What would you have to be sorry about?

MARY. That's not what I mean, I... I mean about your – friend.

CHARLIE. Oh.

(*pause*)

His name was Alan.

MARY. I know his fucking name, Charlie.

(*pause*)

I saw him once, after you left. In the K-mart parking lot. I should have wanted to run him over, or punch

him in the face, but when I went up to him, he was
so – ... He was carrying these bags, he could barely lift
them, he was so thin. Looked like he was about to fall
over. I went up to him with all these amazing things I
was going to say, hurl at him like bricks. And I looked
at him, and I – asked him if he wanted some help. He
let me carry a couple of bags to his car for him, he said
thank you, and I left. I never even told him who I was.

(pause)

When I heard what happened, I thought about coming
by. Bringing Ellie to see you. I should have done that, I
guess, and I'm sorry.

CHARLIE. It's okay. I'd be angry at me too.

(pause)

But thank you. For saying that.

(pause)

MARY. You're wheezing.

CHARLIE. Yeah. It's gotten worse.

MARY. Are you having trouble breathing? Should I call
someone?

CHARLIE. No, it's –

MARY. Let me hear.

*(**MARY** puts her ear to **CHARLIE**'s chest, listening to him
breathe.)*

CHARLIE. How do I sound?

(no response)

Today was the first time we were all together in fifteen
years, you realize that?

(pause)

Back when Ellie was first born, we did that road trip to
the Oregon Coast together. And we stayed in Newport,
and Ellie loved the sand so much. You and I layed on
the beach together, and Ellie played in the surf, and
later that day I went swimming in the ocean. Last time

I ever went swimming, actually. And I kept cutting my legs on the rocks, and the water was so cold, and you were so mad that my legs bled and stained the seats in the minivan. And you said for days after that I smelled like seawater. You remember that?

(**CHARLIE** *puts his hand on* **MARY***'s back as she listens. Silence.*)

MARY. You sound awful.

CHARLIE. I'm dying, Mary.

(**MARY** *looks at him.*)

MARY. Fuck you.

CHARLIE. I'm sorry.

MARY. *Fuck you.*

(*pause*)

For sure?

CHARLIE. Yeah. For sure.

(*pause*)

Listen to me. I need to make certain that Ellie's going to be okay. Beyond the money. She has to have someone around who won't give up on her.

(*pause*)

MARY. You've been eating yourself to death for fifteen years and you're saying that *I* gave up on her?

CHARLIE. I wanted to see her, Mary, I wanted to be a part of your life – both of your lives –

MARY. Go to the hospital, Charlie! You have money, go to the hospital!

CHARLIE. We both know that money is for Ellie. But beyond that, I have to make sure that she's going to be alright, I have to be sure that she's going to have a decent life, where people care for her and she cares for other people – … She doesn't have anyone else, Mary.

MARY. *(grabbing her things)* I have to… I need to go.

CHARLIE. I need to know I did *one thing* right in my life.

(MARY heads to the door. Almost out the door, she stops, not looking at CHARLIE.)

MARY. We both did our parts. I raised her, you're giving her the money. It's the best we could do.

(pause, still not looking at him)

Do you need anything before I leave? Water, or something?

(pause)

CHARLIE. No.

(pause)

MARY. Do you – … Do you want me to help you to the bathroom?

(CHARLIE doesn't respond. MARY waits for a beat, then exits.)

Night.

(CHARLIE is asleep in his wheelchair. His wheezing has gotten much worse, and his breathing is shallow enough that it starts to effect his speech; he often has to pause mid-sentence to take a breath.)

(There is a loud knock at the door, CHARLIE wakes up with start, the sudden movement producing pain in his chest. He winces. Another loud knock.)

CHARLIE. Liz?

ELDER THOMAS. *(offstage)* Can I come inside?

CHARLIE. What the hell are you – ? Are you okay?

ELDER THOMAS. *(offstage)* I'm fine, please let me come inside!

CHARLIE. Yes, just – !

(ELDER THOMAS enters.)

CHARLIE. Are you – ? What's wrong?

ELDER THOMAS. I'm sorry, I'm really, really, really high.

CHARLIE. Why are you high?

ELDER THOMAS. My parents called me tonight.

CHARLIE. So?

ELDER THOMAS. My parents found out where I am. They found out that I'm in Idaho.

CHARLIE. I don't understand.

ELDER THOMAS. Your daughter, she sent pictures of me smoking pot to the mission in Oregon, and told them where I was. And my parents saw the pictures, and they called the church here in town, and they told them where I was staying, and I can't figure out if she was trying to help me or hurt me. Do you ever get that feeling with her?

CHARLIE. I don't. Really understand –

ELDER THOMAS. I thought my parents were going to disown me, and you know what they said? They said they *loved* me, they *cared* about me, and they wanted me to come home. How *awful* is that?

(**CHARLIE** *feels a sharp pain in his chest.*)

ELDER THOMAS. What's wrong?

CHARLIE. I'm fine.

ELDER THOMAS. No, you're not.

CHARLIE. It's just… It's going to go away, it just hurts –

ELDER THOMAS. I just want to help. I know I can help you.

CHARLIE. I'm not going to the hospital –

ELDER THOMAS. I know. I won't make you go. But I can help you.

CHARLIE. Look, just go home to your family, if you need money for a bus or something –

ELDER THOMAS. I know what happened to Alan.

(*pause*)

CHARLIE. What?

ELDER THOMAS. I know what happened that day, at church, the last time he was there.

(*pause*)

I got an e-mail tonight, from Cindy Miller, from the church. She remembers. I had to come tell you right away.

(*silence*)

CHARLIE. What did they do to him?

(*short pause*)

ELDER THOMAS. The talk that day, the talk that his father gave – it was about *Jonah*.

(*pause*)

CHARLIE. What?

ELDER THOMAS. *Jonah and the whale.*

(pause)

Don't you see? That essay you had me read to you –
the one you like so much, the one about *Moby Dick*…
Charlie, I get it now, I understand what God's been
doing with me here, I understand why he sent me
to you, right when you needed help. This isn't just a
coincidence, when I read that e-mail – I knew I was
helping you talk with God. It reaffirmed my faith.

(pause)

Jonah – it's about refusing the call of God, you know?
Jonah tries to escape from God's will, he gets swallowed
by a whale, and when he prays to God for help, God
saves him by making the whale spit him out onto shore.

(silence)

(CHARLIE *laughs a little bit, the laughter causing pain
in his chest.)*

CHARLIE. Is this what it fucking comes down to? I always
thought, whatever they did to him that day must have
been so awful, so cruel… A story? Some stupid *story,*
that's what killed him?

ELDER THOMAS. No, it's *not* a just a story –

CHARLIE. Look, I appreciate what you're trying to do, but
this doesn't mean anything, it – . I don't even know
what I was expecting to find out, it's not –

ELDER THOMAS. *Listen to me.*

(short pause)

Charlie, your boyfriend – he tried to escape God's will,
he chose his lifestyle with you over God. And when he
heard this story, when he heard *God's word,* he knew.
He knew the *truth.* He never prayed for salvation – but
it's not too late for you.

(pause)

CHARLIE. You think Alan died – because he chose to be with me? You think God turned his back on him because he and I were in love?

ELDER THOMAS. *Yes.*

(Silence. **CHARLIE** *stares at him.)*

CHARLIE. You know, I wasn't always this big.

(short pause)

ELDER THOMAS. Yeah, I know –

CHARLIE. I mean, I was never the best looking guy in the room, but – Alan still loved me. He still thought I was beautiful.

ELDER THOMAS. Okay –

CHARLIE. Halfway through the semester, he started meeting me during my office hours – we were both crazy about one another, but we waited until the course was done before we…

ELDER THOMAS. This isn't important –

CHARLIE. It was just after classes had ended for the year, it was a perfect temperature, and we went for a walk in the arboretum. And we kissed.

ELDER THOMAS. Charlie, stop.

CHARLIE. Listen to me. We used to spend entire nights lying next to one another, naked –

ELDER THOMAS. Stop.

CHARLIE. We would make love –

ELDER THOMAS. I don't want to hear about –

CHARLIE. *We would make love.* Do you find that disgusting?

ELDER THOMAS. Charlie, God is ready to help you, you don't have to –

CHARLIE. *I hope there isn't a God.*

(pause)

I hope there isn't a God because I hate thinking that there's an afterlife, that Alan can see what I've done to myself, that he can see my swollen feet, the sores on my skin, the patches of mold in between the flaps –

ELDER THOMAS. Okay, *stop* –

CHARLIE. – the infected ulcers on my ass, the sack of fat on my back that turned brown last year –

ELDER THOMAS. *Stop.*

CHARLIE. This is disgusting?

ELDER THOMAS. YES.

CHARLIE. *I'm* disgusting?

ELDER THOMAS. YES, YOU'RE DISGUSTING, YOU'RE –

(**ELDER THOMAS** *stops himself.*)

(*Long silence.* **CHARLIE** *stares at him.*)

CHARLIE. Go home to your family.

(*Pause.* **ELDER THOMAS** *exits.* **CHARLIE** *breathes heavily, wheezing, trying to calm himself down.*)

(*The lights quickly snap to black.*)

(*In the darkness, the waves are heard once again – this time definite, sharp, and aggressive, rising quickly in volume until lights rise on:*)

FRIDAY

Morning.

(CHARLIE, at his computer, speaking into a microphone. A small web cam rests next to his laptop, not hooked up. CHARLIE is noticeably weaker, and is having trouble maintaining his line of thought.)

CHARLIE. So, here we are. Your complaints have been heard. The powers that be have decided to replace me with someone else – someone more "stable" and "traditional" as the e-mail to me said. This person will no doubt make you rewrite and rewrite and rewrite, just like I did for seventeen years, analyzing every word, every punctuation mark for clarity and precision of meaning, and...

(pause)

You all sent me your essays. Your new essays, the ones you didn't rewrite. The ones you didn't think about, and...

(CHARLIE types for a second, pulling up something on his computer.)

KristyStar9, you wrote: "My parents want me to be a radiologist, but I don't even know what that is." Peter6969, you wrote: "I'm sick of people telling me that I have promise." AdamD567, about two pages in, you wrote: "I think I need to accept that my life isn't going to be very exciting." You all wrote these – *amazing*, things, I just –

(pause)

CHARLIE. *(cont.)* I want to be honest with you now. I've been just a voice to all of you all semester, and now you've been so honest with me, I just...

(CHARLIE pauses, then plugs the web cam into his computer. He stares at it for a second. He moves the camera away from him, then tilts it down, filming his body. He brings the camera back up to his face.)

These assignments – they don't matter. This course doesn't matter. College doesn't matter. These beautiful, honest things you wrote – they matter.

(CHARLIE pauses a second, then throws his computer and the camera across the room. They crash against the wall.)

Afternoon.

(CHARLIE is sitting in his wheelchair. LIZ stands in the doorway, staring at the broken computer, holding her bag.)

CHARLIE. I'm sorry.

LIZ. Don't.

(LIZ makes her way inside, closes the door slowly. She moves over to CHARLIE.)

CHARLIE. Liz –

LIZ. I said don't.

(LIZ stares at him for a second. She reaches into her bag, pulling out a stethoscope. She puts it on, then moves toward CHARLIE, putting it on his chest.)

Breathe in.

(CHARLIE breathes in.)

LIZ. More.

CHARLIE. I can't. Hurts.

(LIZ takes the stethoscope off, puts it back in her bag. She looks at CHARLIE.)

LIZ. I really hate you for putting me through this again, you know that?

(pause)

Those last few months before Alan… And I'd come over here, and I'd scream at him, shake him. For God's sake, eat something! You stupid piece of shit, you just need to eat something!

(pause)

I'd come back and the food would be gone. Not because he ate it – but because he hid it somewhere. Threw it out the window, fed it to the neighbor's dog. You were beside yourself, had no idea what to do… God, that was awful.

CHARLIE. It was awful for me, too.

LIZ. Well, you weren't the one who found him. In your bed, underneath the covers, curled up like a fetus. God, you think you only see things like that in documentaries.

*(**LIZ** reaches into her bag, taking out two sub sandwiches.)*

I got you two meatball subs. Extra cheese. I don't know what I'm doing.

(pause)

You have money. You need to go to the hospital.

(pause)

CHARLIE. No.

LIZ. For me. Go to the hospital for me.

CHARLIE. No.

(pause)

LIZ. How *dare* you do this to me again?!

*(Silence. **CHARLIE**'s breathing is increasingly shallow.)*

(The sound of waves from before is heard at a very low level, steadily increasing in volume as the scene progresses.)

CHARLIE. She helped him.

LIZ. What?

CHARLIE. She wasn't trying to hurt him. She was trying to help him.

LIZ. Who are you talking about?

CHARLIE. The Mormon kid. He's going home. She did that. She wasn't trying to hurt him.

LIZ. Oh, God, Charlie?

CHARLIE. She didn't do it to hurt him, she did it to send him home.

LIZ. Do you feel light-headed? Charlie, look at me.

CHARLIE. She was trying to help him!

LIZ. Who?!

CHARLIE. Ellie. She was trying to help him, she just wanted him to go home.

LIZ. Oh my God. You need – . I don't know what to do, I can't help you!

(CHARLIE looks at LIZ.)

CHARLIE. Do you ever get the feeling. That people. Are incapable. Of not caring? People. Are. Amazing.

(ELLIE charges in through the front door holding the essay from before. She stops when she sees CHARLIE, looking at him for a brief moment.)

ELLIE. What's wrong with him?

LIZ. He's dying.

(pause)

ELLIE. So call someone.

CHARLIE. No.

ELLIE. Call an ambulance.

CHARLIE. No. Liz. Please don't.

ELLIE. Call a fucking ambulance!

(LIZ takes her cell phone out.)

CHARLIE. Liz. Please.

LIZ. No. I'm not letting this go on any more, I'm calling an ambulance. I'm not going through this again!

ELLIE. I need to talk to him.

(LIZ starts dialing.)

LIZ. So talk.

ELLIE. Alone.

LIZ. I'm not leaving you alone with him.

ELLIE. I need to talk to him alone!

CHARLIE. Liz. Please.

(LIZ looks at him. Pause.)

LIZ. Fine. I'm calling an ambulance, and I'm waiting downstairs. We'll get you to the hospital, and you're *going to be fine.* You understand me?

(**LIZ** *exits.*)

ELLIE. What's wrong with you?

CHARLIE. I can't. Breathe very well.

(*pause*)

ELLIE. The ambulance is coming. They'll take you to the hospital, you should have gone a while ago.

(*pause*)

Why did you do that?!

CHARLIE. What?

(**ELLIE** *holds up the essay.*)

ELLIE. I failed.

CHARLIE. It's. A really good essay.

ELLIE. No, it's not a really good essay! I failed!

(*pause*)

Are you just trying to screw me over one last time before you die? I don't care that you're dying! I don't care about you! Do you want me to fail out of high school, is that why you did this?

CHARLIE. I didn't. Write it.

ELLIE. This is the essay you gave me yesterday.

CHARLIE. You didn't. Read it.

ELLIE. I don't need to read it, it got an F!

CHARLIE. Read it.

(**ELLIE** *looks at the paper for a second.*)

ELLIE. This is… I know what this is.

CHARLIE. I knew you would. You never. Forget anything.

ELLIE. I wrote this.

(*pause*)

I wrote this in eighth grade for English, why do you – ?

CHARLIE. And I felt saddest of all. When I read the boring chapters. That were only descriptions of whales.

Because I knew. That the author was just trying to save us. From his own sad story. Just for a little while.

ELLIE. Why do you have this?

CHARLIE. Your mother. She sent it to me. Four years ago. I wanted to know how you were doing. In school. So she sent it. And it's the best essay. I've ever read.

(*pause*)

ELLIE. Why are you fucking with me like this?

CHARLIE. I'm not.

(*pause*)

You're so beautiful. Ellie, you're beautiful.

ELLIE. Stop saying that.

CHARLIE. You're amazing. This essay. Is amazing.

ELLIE. Stop saying that!

CHARLIE. You're the best thing. I've ever done.

(**CHARLIE** *has a severe chest pain, he doubles over.*)

(**ELLIE** *is frantic.*)

ELLIE. What's the matter?!

CHARLIE. Ellie.

ELLIE. I can't be here right now, I have to go, I can't –

CHARLIE. You're perfect. You'll be happy. You'll care for people.

ELLIE. The ambulance is coming, they'll help you!

CHARLIE. No. They won't.

(*pause*)

ELLIE. *You're going to the hospital.*

CHARLIE. No.

ELLIE. You just need surgery or something!

CHARLIE. Read it to me.

ELLIE. What?!

CHARLIE. If you want to help. Read it to me. You can help me. If you read it.

(**ELLIE** *is holding back tears at this point.*)

ELLIE. You asshole. You fat fucking asshole!

CHARLIE. You'll help. If you read it.

ELLIE. Fuck you.

CHARLIE. Please.

ELLIE. Fuck you!

CHARLIE. Ellie.

ELLIE. Dad, *please.*

(*Pause.* **ELLIE** *looks at* **CHARLIE**, *pleading.* **ELLIE** *and* **CHARLIE** *are in the same position as they were in their first scene together. The sound of waves gets louder and louder.*)

(*reading*) "In the amazing book *Moby Dick* by the author Herman Melville, the author recounts his story of being at sea. In the first part of his book, the author, calling himself Ishmael, is in a small sea-side town and he is sharing a bed with a man named Queequeg."

(**CHARLIE** *smiles at* **ELLIE** *through the pain. He reaches up and takes the oxygen tube out of his nose.*)

"The author and Queequeg go to church and hear a sermon about Jonah, and later set out on a ship captained by the pirate named Ahab, who is missing a leg, and very much wants to kill the whale which is named Moby Dick, and which is white."

(**CHARLIE** *braces himself on his wheelchair.*)

"In the course of the book, the pirate Ahab encounters many hardships. His entire life is set around trying to kill a certain whale."

(*Wheezing heavily and with a huge amount of effort and pain,* **CHARLIE** *manages to stand up.*)

"I think this is sad because this whale doesn't have any emotions, and doesn't know how bad Ahab wants to kill him."

(CHARLIE, staring at ELLIE, manages to take one step forward. His breathing becomes quicker. The waves are louder still.)

ELLIE. *(cont.)* "He's just a poor big animal. And I feel bad for Ahab as well, because he thinks that his life will be better if he can kill this whale, but in reality it won't help him at all."

(CHARLIE takes another step. His breathing is more and more rapid.)

"I was very saddened by this book, and I felt many emotions for the characters."

(Another step.)

"And I felt saddest of all when I read the boring chapters that were only descriptions of whales, because I knew that the author was just trying to save us from his own sad story, just for a little while."

(CHARLIE takes one last step toward ELLIE. The waves reach their loudest level.)

"This book made me think about my own life, and then it made me feel glad for my – "

(CHARLIE looks up. The waves cut off.)

(A sharp intake of breath. The lights snap to black.)

End of Play.

CPSIA information can be obtained
at www.ICGtesting.com
Printed in the USA
LVOW10s0523070217
523432LV00006B/21/P